D1765790

The Chase

Tracey Chizoba Fletcher

Published by PabPub, 2021.

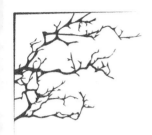

THE PLAN

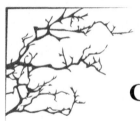

CHAPTER ONE

It started in a bar; a ramshackle of some sorts, barely hanging to life, by a corner of Ijeromi Street. It was shoddily built with bits and pieces of loose plank, hastily put together, and an ancient-looking rusted roof hanging over it like a dark cloud. The picture was a sore sight to the eyes; clearly uninviting and unappealing. Passersby always wondered who in their right minds would want to relax in such an appalling establishment. Yes, an establishment it was! If anyone managed to stand still for up to a minute and stare fixedly at the writing on the outside, even with some of the letters missing, you could clearly make out: MAMA NONSO'S DRINKING ESTABLISHMENT etched on it.

This bar that people seemed to despise was Mama Nonso's heaven on earth. It was her greatest achievement till date and she was incredibly proud of it. Why wouldn't she be? It was the only thing that she had birthed and brought to life. You would wonder, what of her son? Wasn't she Mama Nonso? We would get to that.

CHAPTER TWO

You see, Mama Nonso was first by name Chikodi. Right from a very young age, she realized all was not well with her family. Her parents didn't act like others. But you couldn't blame them? Chikodi's parents hadn't planned to have her. They were neighbours in their twenty room compound in Mushin. Both squatters in fact! A few heated glances passed between them, and they began having romps in which ever room was vacant. They were so intoxicated with each other's bodies that the thought of the consequences of their action did not cross their mind.

When Chikodi's mother woke up one morning and rushed outside the room to throw up, her fellow tenants watched her with scorn. They had turned a blind eye to the escapades of the two lovers, but now they wondered what the two idle lovers would make of their situation.

Their hosts were upset to say the least over their actions and quickly asked them to take leave of their rooms. They cried and threw their bodies on the ground, rolling and begging to be allowed to stay; but their pleas fell on deaf ears. Their meagre belongings were thrown out and they were chased out the gate. The two hosts felt no remorse over what they had done but instead felt sorry for the unborn child. The child couldn't have had a more unsuitable choice as parents.

CHAPTER THREE

How the two lovers managed to get their act together was a miracle! They moved to a new area where no one knew them, and slept on the street. Their situation was a poor sight to behold. As the woman's belly extended, people came together and rented a room for them. The two lovers had the foresight to behave well so that people were moved to assist them further and plied them with gifts such as: baby clothes, baby bath, et cetera. When the baby was born, gifts of money were equally presented, while the father was given the job of a security man by a kind landlord on their street. They became Papa and Mama Chikodi.

Chikodi was just approaching nine months when the wool was lifted off the eyes of those who knew her parents. Papa and Mama Chikodi had soon grown tired of pretending to be who they were not. Firstly, Mama Chikodi's body which had symbolized a haven of beauty to Papa Chikodi had soon lost its glow in his eyes after the birth of Chikodi. She was now old chassis. He needed something fresh. His salary provided him a leeway to indulge his desires.

When Mama Chikodi realized this, she sought revenge by taking on an affair with the married man who lived three rooms away from hers. Her neighbour reveled in her body. One man's meat was another man's poison, wasn't it? It didn't take long for disaster to strike.

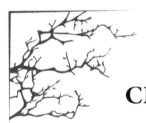

CHAPTER FOUR

The married man's wife caught wind of the affair and all hell broke loose. The two women fought to the teeth and came away with bloody injuries. A truce had to be called in. Mama Chikodi was forced to steer clear of the man but that didn't stop her adulterous behaviour. She had just begun.

Papa Chikodi didn't fare better, either. His lackadaisical attitude cost him his job. Life at home was hell. He was constantly at loggerheads with his wife. A day after Chikodi clocked two, her mother picked up her handbag on the pretext of going to the market. She never came back. Her father begrudged the act of being a single parent and failed to live up to his expectations as a father. The only thing he succeeded in doing was always been able to pay the rent. He never wanted to sleep on the streets again.

The mothers in the compound made a collective effort to train Chikodi. They fed her and took care of her. She grew up under their guardianship. Mama Ebuka paid her the closest attention and was proud of the fact that Chikodi was turning out to be a good child.

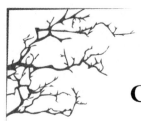

CHAPTER FIVE

When Chikodi was fourteen, she began to blossom as a woman. Her breasts stood firm and her hips grew wider. Her size masked her age, though. She also began to comprehend the power of a woman. We could rightly say that even under the power of good mentorship, Chikodi still fell victim to the claws of her genes. The same blood of her parents coursed through her veins. Who would fall under her trap? None other than the husband of Mama Ebuka. An outright betrayal!

When Mama Ebuka found out, she warned Chikodi never to come near her. It spelled doom for Chikodi because the other women in the compound and their children steered clear of her. Their friendship had been a fortress for her. Now, she understood the meaning of been alone. One morning a week after the warning, just like her mother, Chikodi picked up a bag, bigger than the one her mother had left with twelve years ago, and left the compound.

Her womanly powers came in handy as finding a place for herself was no big issue. A young man who met her at a bus-stop happily took her in. A month after, Chikodi realized she was pregnant. It was for Mama Ebuka's husband.

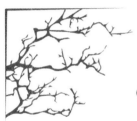

CHAPTER SIX

The young man accepted the pregnancy. He was drunk with Chikodi's body and warning bells didn't ring in his head. Chikodi carried the pregnancy up to full term. On the day of labour, she writhed and groaned in pain. It was the hardest thing she had ever done. She had decided that if it was a boy, he would be called Nonso. The child was born, but unfortunately he died after twenty-four hours.

In a funny twist, she called herself 'Mama Nonso'. He would be the only child she ever bore. Mama Nonso moved from man to man and lived a rough life. At thirty-five, she looked sixty. After another failed relationship, she decided to do something with herself. The only thing that came to her mind was to sell alcoholic drinks.

She had started off with selling alcoholic sachet drinks. And now here she was with her bar. It was her paradise. Something she had done on her own.

CHAPTER SEVEN

The atmosphere was humid and the air still. Even the standing fan was giving off hot air. What was worse was that the atmosphere was laced with the acrid smell of restlessness and hopelessness that hung around Bunmi and Yusuf. They sat stiffly in the armless plastic chairs, round a plastic table while Mama Nonso scurried to attend to their needs – a keg of palm wine and a plate of ponmo. They were the only customers.

They remained silent until Mama Nonso placed their requests on the table. She went outside to grant them privacy but she could hear everything they said. That was her secret.

After two cups of palm wine each, their tongues were set loose. It was time to grumble and complain about the state of their affairs.

Bunmi let off a loud hiccup before launching his tirade. "I don tire for this country o! Na suffer suffer we dey do for here."

Yusuf mirrored his thoughts. "Baba Fela don talk am na! Na suffer suffer for work! You go suffer find work, suffer do the work, suffer spend de money. You go dey cry as you dey spend am. At the end of the day, you no go see wetin you use the money do o!" he chorused.

Mama Nonso brought out her plastic fan. It was going to be a long day.

CHAPTER EIGHT

At about five p.m., Bunmi and Yusuf had done justice to the keg of palm wine. They pulled their money together and paid Mama Nonso who pleaded with them to come back the next day. She happily escorted them out the shop and watched them leave as they sang loudly and swayed dangerously.

The duo drew the attention of people as they picked their way to the abode of their mutual friend, Chima. They walked right into his room and found him stretched on the bed, laid out on the floor. A bottle of Heineken sat undisturbed at the foot of his bed. He was deep in sleep.

Both of them fell on top of him. Chima quickly roused from his sleep

"Why una dey disturb me na? You no go allow me sleep. You think say to do watchman for night na easy job?" Chima berated in a groggy voice.

Yusuf hissed loudly while Bunmi countered him. "Dat one na work! Abeg make we hear word."

"Is that what you would say?" Chima asked, rising up from the bed.

"Yes!" Bunmi answered in between hiccups, and closed his eyes.

Chima sighed quietly and picked up his bucket by the corner of the room. He needed to get prepared for work.

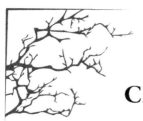

CHAPTER NINE

Chima was checking his torchlight when Yusuf stirred from his sleep. The hands on the clock showed seven p.m.

"It's good you have woken up! I need to go to work," Chima said. "There is Eba and soup in the cupboard for the both of you. I would be back in the morning."

"Thanks, man," Yusuf said, as he yawned loudly. Chima was already at the door when Yusuf's voice stopped him.

"What is it? I'm almost running late," Chima said.

Yusuf stood beside him. "Chima, you are the man! You are the brain amongst us. Find a way, eh. Find us a way to make some money. We can't continue this way; you a watchman, Bunmi and me barely managing to survive. We need a plan, man. Please, come up with something before we die here," Yusuf pleaded, desperation written all over his face.

Chima sighed. "I don think tire. My head wan bursting from thinking. I no know wetin to think again."

"Just try one more time, eh. Something may come up," Yusuf pressed further.

Chima stared straight ahead, lost in thought. A few minutes later, he turned to Yusuf, gave a silent nod, and stepped out of the room.

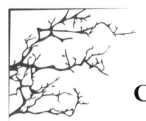

CHAPTER TEN

In another part of town, two men whose paths would cross unknowingly to them, in bizarre circumstances, were both hanging out at a bar. The bar was quite cozy with vinyl topped seats and neatly shined tables. They were both sitting a few metres apart, immersed in their phones, and thoughts.

The middle-aged man had a bottle of star and a glass cup on his table. The beer was untouched. His gaze was focused on his phone on the table. He was waiting for a call. A call that would change his life.

The younger man, about twenty-three by the looks of him had his bottle of Guinness opened, with a half-empty cup beside him. He was equally waiting for a call. A call that would make him happy. He was trying to while away the time and keep his anxiety at bay by flipping through pictures on his Instagram profile.

Suddenly, the sound of a ringtone rang in the air. The two men looked at their phones. Their calls had come in.

The middle-aged man clicked 'Accept' with his heart hammering in his chest. The young man received the call, willing his desire to come true.

CHAPTER ELEVEN

The middle aged-man, Anthony, listened to the voice on the other end. He felt his heart leap. His heart desire would soon be fulfilled. All that was left was a text message.

Dapo was overjoyed at the turn of the conversation. He ended the call with a promise to see the caller the next day.

The two men got up and paid their bills. Anthony paid cash while Dapo used the POS machine. Each left the bar with their hearts racing. Anthony made it to his car-a 2015 corolla-and quickly drove off. Dapo hailed a bike. His car was parked at home. His house was just around the corner.

CHAPTER TWELVE

A nthony arrived home to the sweet embrace of his wife Sarah. She met him at the door and wrapped her arms around him. This was her daily ritual of welcoming him. It never stopped to reawaken his love for her. When he stared down into her eyes, he knew that he made the right choice marrying her. Their love had grown strong even after ten years of marriage wrought with challenges, some very recently. That's why the call this evening had given him some form of hope. Perhaps they could rise up again. All he needed to do was get Sarah to accept what he needed to do. Her consent was very important to him.

The kids – nine-year-old Diana and seven-year-old Bobby - had already gone to sleep. Anthony had gotten home at some minutes past eight p.m. It was a rule for the children to be on their beds by eight on the dot.

After having his dinner of Semovita with Egusi soup, Anthony retired to the bedroom. He had an ice-cold bath, and sat up in bed, waiting for his wife. When Sarah sauntered in, he knew it was time. This would be the toughest appeal he would ever give.

CHAPTER THIRTEEN

D apo ambled into his one-room self-contained apartment, ecstatic. His lifelong dream would be a reality in just a few days. Yes, it was a crazy idea, but Dapo had always wanted to do things differently. He was a hopeless romantic. His friends called him words like: Eccentric. Their endless teasing never got to him. He loved to be the one different person in a group of hundreds, thousands, and even millions.

He simply loved the sense of adventure. The photo albums he had carefully tucked in his bedside drawer was a testament to that. It contained pictures of the various visits he had made so far. He had ticked off visits to the Obudu Mountain Resort in Cross Rivers State, Yankari Game Reserve in Bauchi State, Olumo Rock in Ogun state, the Hill of Idanre in Ondo State, and even the popular Calabar festival, to name a few.

What was stranger was that Dapo undertook these visits all by himself! But the status quo was about to change.

This would be the first time he would include someone else in his plans. A person so dear to his heart that the feeling sometimes overwhelmed him. And this was why this particular adventure was so special. He needed to get this right. It was time to conclude his plans since the nod to move ahead had come.

CHAPTER FOURTEEN

C hima arrived at his post, a few minutes late. The man whose place he was to take hung out with him for a bit as he filled him in on the latest developments. When the man had departed, Chima went round the property, trying to ascertain if everything was in place.

The property belonged to the only paint factory in the area. It employed most of the youths in the vicinity, thereby taking them off the street, and providing them with a staple income. Chima worked in the security department. The men took shifts so as to stay fresh and alert. It was Chima's turn to work nights from Sunday to Thursday.

When he was satisfied with his search, he took up position in the Security room. The screens stared at him as the CCTV cameras outside displayed what was happening. It was going to be a long night. He equally had more than enough time to think.

CHAPTER FIFTEEN

Anthony and Sarah were again in each other's embrace, having quenched their thirst for each other. Anthony knew Sarah would soon be drifting off to sleep. It was time to talk.

"Honey," he nudged her, "we need to talk."

Sarah wriggled in his arms. "I am so tired. Please, can't it wait till tomorrow?"

"No, please. We need to talk now."

Even in Sarah's foggy state, the weight in his words pierced through her mind. She wearily sat up and fixed her gaze on his face which had now taken on a solemn, serious expression.

Anthony held her hands in his, took a deep breath, and began. "Honey, I bless God for giving me a wife like you. You have been there for me through thick and thin. Since I lost my job at the bank two years ago, you have held the fort without murmuring or complaining. You treat the stipends I bring in as if it were millions. You haven't stopped honouring me.

"You are aware that I have been praying and trying all I can to improve our situation. Your teaching job isn't fetching enough anymore in relation to our increased spending. I need to be the man that I should." His voice quavered at this point and Sarah saw an opportunity to chip in something.

"Honey, I know how you feel. You know I will always be here for you. I just completed a seven days prayer. I am sure that an answer to our problems will come soon."

Anthony held her gaze. "What if an answer has already come?"

Sarah looked flustered. "What do you mean?"

"I met Paul three days ago. We sort of ran into each other. He told me about an opening and I indicated interest. He got back to me today."

Sarah's eyes grew wide.

"I have got a job, Sarah!"

A loud whoop of excitement rented the air as Sarah embraced him, before jumping out of the bed, and running circles round the room, with her hands stretched towards the heavens. It took a little while before Sarah realized that Anthony wasn't celebrating like she was. "What is it?" she asked, alarmed.

CHAPTER SIXTEEN

This was definitely the hard part.

"Honey, please come and sit," Anthony beckoned to Sarah.

"What is it?" Sarah asked, again.

Anthony chose his words carefully as she sat beside him. "Yes, I got a job. It is not a regular nine to five job. You see Paul knows some big men. Very wealthy men! They need an Accountant with my experience to help them transfer some funds. These men live very secretive lives. I can help them with this. The offer is..."

Sarah cut him short. "What did you say, Anthony? You want to get involved in shady dealings! How could you say that this is an answer from God? Is it not money they may have gotten fraudulently that you want to help them hide? Honey, I know things are tough but we can still manage," she said.

"No! No!" Anthony said, rising. "I'm tired of the management. We can't continue like this, living from hand to mouth. Listen, Sarah, the offer is for five million. Five million! It could change our financial situation."

"Did you hear yourself, Anthony? It could change our financial situation! But at what price? We have preached truth and honesty to our children. How would we look them in the face if you do this? No, honey, I won't support this."

They stared at each other, the fight still evident in their eyes. It wasn't over yet.

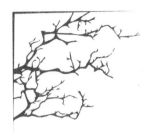

CHAPTER
SEVENTEEN

Anthony's voice took on an edge he didn't wish to have. "The children don't need to know. I am the head of this home. My wife and children need me to begin taking care of responsibilities. Can't you see that I can't even look my children in the face because I can't sufficiently provide for them? This is an opportunity for me to be whole again."

Anthony drew closer to his wife. "Please Sarah, I can't do this myself. I need your support. We need to have our lives back. We would spend the money judiciously and open a business for ourselves. We need to live a better life. I promise that I won't take another job after this. Please, do this for us. Let me do it," he pleaded.

Sarah was lost in the pleading in his eyes and soft, fierceness in his voice. She found her resistance crumbling. "Please, just this once, okay."

"Just this once," he promised, as they shared a deep kiss.

"So when do you get it done?" Sarah asked, after they had broken away from the kiss.

"I await a text message tomorrow. It will let me know when it would be."

Anthony turned off the light as they lay down to sleep, different thoughts heavy on their minds.

CHAPTER EIGHTEEN

C hima returned the next morning just as Bunmi and Yusuf were rousing from sleep. He was too tired to hold a conversation.

"Guys, let's meet up by four at Mama Nonso's. We have something to talk about," he intimated them.

"Wow! Chima, have you come up with something?" Yusuf asked, excitedly.

"Come up with what?" Bunmi asked, in confusion.

Chima had drifted off to sleep without answering them. Yusuf dragged Bunmi outside to reveal to him the discussion that had taken place the previous night.

CHAPTER NINETEEN

By four p.m. that evening, Chima sauntered into Mama Nonso's place. His friends were already seated, waiting for him.

"Chima, my man!" they both hailed him as he settled down to sit with them. Mama Nonso clearly pleased with their visit and the money that would come from their spending, placed an extra cup on the table for Chima. He poured out some of the palm wine, took a sip, and sighed in contentment.

"Mama Nonso, you are the best!" he drawled. "You always have the real stuff."

Mama Nonso laughed loudly. "Only the best for my customers!" She left to sit outside, giving them their privacy.

"What's the deal? What have you thought of, bro?" Yusuf asked, anxiously.

Chima stared at them intensely over the rim of his glass. "It isn't about what I have come up with. The question is if you both are ready for this?"

Bunmi and Yusuf turned towards each other, a dazed look in their eyes. The question had sounded like a death sentence.

CHAPTER TWENTY

After both men had convinced Chima of their willingness to do whatever was needed to be done, Chima felt obliged to speak.

"We are all aware that we can't make money in this country if we decide to be good. Being good doesn't pay here. Only the hard-hearted make it here. We need to be like them. The rich are busy stealing our money and transferring it to foreign accounts for their children while we keep suffering. We need to get that money back. It's ours. We are only taking back what is rightfully ours," he stated with a glint in his eyes.

Bunmi found his voice then. "Are you saying we steal? Turn to thieves?"

Chima stood up angrily. "No, we aren't stealing. We are taking what is ours. Do you understand that? If you don't, then I would walk away."

Yusuf quickly jumped in, after throwing a warning look at Bunmi. "No man, don't say that! We are good. You know you are our brain. We are the muscle. Just tell us what we need to do, okay."

Chima sat back down. "This is the plan: We are going to pretend to be police officers. We would get the uniforms and mount a stake out. Someone is definitely going to fall into our trap."

They all wore serious looks now.

"Aren't we missing something? Where is the location?" Bunmi asked, with his brows furrowed in puzzlement.

Chima replied, "The road to Crystal Heights Hotel! We strike on Friday."

Today was Tuesday. They had three days to get prepared.

CHAPTER TWENTY-ONE

C rystal Heights Hotel had opened to a lot of noise and aplomb six months ago. It was a state of the art edifice, with a five star rating. The owner wasn't known; but it was widely rumoured that it belonged to a wealthy politician who had contracted the construction of the building and its interior decoration to Arabs. In three months, a glass-like edifice, with ultra-modern facilities, was ready to be opened to the world.

The air of mystery surrounding the hotel was also as a result of its location. You had to drive past Ajah, be on your way to Sangotedo, make a couple of turns that had you drive along a lonely stretch that was surrounded by trees on both sides of the road, before you drove up a hill, with the vision of the hotel looming large at the top of the hill. The hotel shone in the distance; hence the name: Crystal Heights Hotel.

Thus you could say that the journey to the hotel, coupled with the scenery before the arrival, and the feeling of travelling to a different place, held a mystique that drew people in their droves, and that was why it had scored a huge success within a short time after opening.

CHAPTER TWENTY-TWO

A knock at the door had Dapo scrambling to his feet, thereby up-turning the contents on his work table, as sheets of paper and a pen, clattered to the ground. He opened the door, and smiled broadly at his guest.

"Come in, Darling," he said, as he kissed her, "I've been expecting you."

Deola gave a loud chuckle as she padded into his room and found the place a mess. "What is going on here?" she asked.

"Sorry darling," Dapo said, as he picked sheets of paper off the couch and made space for her to sit.

"What is going on, Dapo?" Deola asked. Why all these?"

Dapo sat beside her. "Darling, you know how much I love you! I have to make sure that our outing this Friday is perfect. I can't afford mistakes. So I am writing down all I think we would need."

"Okay," Deola said, nodding her head. "But it's just a camping trip, right? As crazy as it sounds, and I still can't believe I agreed to this, coming in here and seeing all this, is making me feel like maybe it's a little too much. How about just a trip to the beach?" she asked, anxiously.

"No, it is okay, babe. I got this, okay. Maybe I am overdoing it, with all these papers," he said, as he laughed loud. "This camp trip is happening this Friday. Now get up, and let's look at my plans."

They got up and picked their way to his work table, heads bowed over his plans.

CHAPTER TWENTY-THREE

It was Wednesday and the call hadn't come through, yet. Anthony didn't want to come out as been desperate, so he had held back from calling his friend. Since Monday, it had been torture to breathe, eat, or think. All he pictured in his mind was the money. Five million was no joke. The call had to come through.

Anthony was just getting out of his car when his phone rang. He looked at the screen. His heart skipped a beat.

"Hello," he said.

"The deal is on. Friday it is."

Anthony got to the door. Sarah was waiting for him. "I got the call," he said as he returned her hug. "All is set for Friday."

Anthony felt his wife's body stiffen. He gently rubbed his hands over her back. "It's going to be fine, darling. I promise you that."

Sarah's answer was burrowing deeper into his embrace.

THE EXECUTION

CHAPTER TWENTY-FOUR

Since the day Chima had unveiled the plan, it had been a rush to put things in place. Bunmi and Yusuf had jumped on the bandwagon, playing their parts, in order to set the wheels in motion.

Bunmi and Yusuf paid a visit to a fashion designer, to make their request. Baba Lateef had no scruples giving them what they needed, as long as his hands were greased. By Thursday when they returned to his shop, the uniforms were ready.

"Baba Lateef, you try o!" Bunmi hailed him. "No difference between wetin you sew and original police uniform, o! Yusuf, can't you see it?" he asked, as he stretched out the uniform for Yusuf to take a proper look.

"Baba Lateef, you be correct man!" Yusuf said, liking what he saw.

Baba Lateef got up from behind his sewing machine. His eyes always glistened with pleasure whenever he was praised for his work. It was his pride. But now, his eyes took on a serious expression. "Listen the both of you," he said, pointing at them, "I sewed these uniforms in the dead of the night so no one would see me. I sent my apprentices away today, so they wouldn't see you. I am not interested in what you intend to do with these uniforms, but know these, I have never seen you both. Do you understand?"

What he meant sank into the minds of the pair. They suddenly felt foolish. Yusuf moved the uniforms into the bag they had come with. "Sure, Baba Lateef, we have never met." They both walked away, their heads bowed.

CHAPTER TWENTY-FIVE

C hima was waiting for them in his room. He inspected the uniforms, and was quite satisfied with it.

"It is only a retired police officer, or one who is already in the force, that can spot the difference. Baba Lateef delivered well on this."

Bunmi and Yusuf sat down on the mattress, breathing a sigh of relief. They had fulfilled their part of the bargain.

Chima opened the drawer by the side of the bed, and brought out three batons. He handed two batons to the pair. "These are yours. I don't think they would be missed at the factory."

Yusuf held his, with a huge smirk on his face. "We are now proper police officers. All that is left is a gun."

Bunmi reacted instantaneously. "Don't say that again? We don't have to kill anybody."

"I never said we would kill anyone. It is just to even out the look," Yusuf retorted.

Chima held his palms up. "We don't have to argue. Hopefully, the sight of our uniforms and batons would scare those wealthy brats, and spur them to release whatever we ask," he said, diluting the tension. "As for the Hilux van, I would pick it up tomorrow from my Uncle's house. When he gave me the keys two weeks ago to his compound, to look it up from time to time, I never knew that it would be a solution to our problem. Guys, we are covered. Tomorrow, we strike."

The trio retreated into their minds; as they prepared for the D-day.

CHAPTER TWENTY-SIX

D eola lay sprawled on the couch. Dapo was standing by his work table, a sheet in one hand, and a pen in the other. He crossed things off on the paper as he spoke.

"Tent, present. Canned food, water, torchlights, power banks, sweaters, socks, sleeping bags..."

"Darling, why don't you come over here?" Deola called. "You have been over the list a trillion times. Let it rest. You could go over it in the morning. Drop the list, and come here."

Dapo sat on the floor. "Okay, here I am. What do we do now? I feel empty without that list," he stated.

"Why don't we watch a movie? Yes, let's have a feel of what it means to live in the city before we get lost in the wilds," Deola said, jokingly.

"We won't get lost, Deola. As long as I am here with you, nothing bad would happen. This would be a weekend you would never forget. That is a promise."

He laid a kiss on her forehead.

CHAPTER TWENTY-SEVEN

The night had been tense. Sleep was far way. They had both tossed and turned, the sheets entangled, and soaked through with their stale sweat. The morning had them looking tired, with heavily-lidded eyes. They both avoided communication as much as they could.

On the way out to their separate destinations, Anthony held his wife by the hand. "It shouldn't be this way. Tonight, we celebrate. Let's have a treat. Take the kids to the Eatery by the school after you are through with your teaching lessons. I would pick you up from there, okay."

Sarah swallowed a huge lump of saliva. "All right. Good luck!"

She wished she could say more, but she couldn't find the words. She kissed him, and held the kids, as they walked the short distance to school.

CHAPTER TWENTY-EIGHT

I t was 3:45 p.m. The boot of the car and the passenger seats were filled with all that they needed for the trip. Dapo was making his last trip from the house with an armful of packages. A few toppled to the ground in his haste. Deola laughed loudly. Dapo feigned annoyance.

"Is it my fault that I want to make sure we leave with everything?" he asked.

"No, my love. You just look like Father Christmas bearing his gifts."

Dapo had to laugh at that.

"Please hurry up, darling. We need to leave quickly so we can get to our destination, and unpack, before it gets late."

"This is the last trip," Dapo said. He got behind the steering wheel, revved up the engine, and zoomed away.

The trip had begun.

CHAPTER TWENTY-NINE

C hima, Bunmi, and Yusuf stared at their reflections in the mirror. They were pleased with what they saw. Chima had made the decision for them to move to his Uncle's house in one of the under-developed estates along Lekki-Epe expressway. The house was a sprawling mansion, with a high gate, and a barbed wire around the fence. It was one of three buildings, on a close, with a lot of space between the buildings. Security was lax in the estate, thus, their activity couldn't be monitored by anyone.

Chima had argued that his one-room apartment couldn't afford them such level of privacy. Dressing up in a police uniform, and zooming off in a black Hilux van would have certainly raised eyebrows.

The building was luxurious enough, with all the necessary comforts to suppress their anxiety, and calm their frayed nerves. Now, they stood before the mirror, men on a mission.

Chima looked at his wristwatch. "It is four p.m. In thirty minutes, we take our leave," he announced.

CHAPTER THIRTY

For the umpteenth time, Sarah stared at her phone. The meat pie and bottle of coke she had purchased for herself sat untouched on the table. The animated chatter coming from Diana and Bobby was lost on her. The children were excited to be somewhere else apart from the house and the school. They happily munched on their snacks as they tried to draw their mother into their conversation.

Sarah sat restless. Anthony had promised to call her. She had to wait. She had to trust the man she married. He had never failed her. She quickly pulled up the memory of the first time they had met. They were both serving out their one year mandatory NYSC service at Maiduguri. In their uniforms, they had boarded the same bus and conversation had been easy. They had become fast friends, being in each other's company as often as possible. It hadn't taken them long to realize they loved each other. It wasn't the passionate, butterfly in my stomach kind of love! It was a reassuring, guaranteed feeling of mutual respect and commitment they felt for each other. Since then they had been each other's back bone, and the years of marriage hadn't dulled the love they felt for each other. Yes, she would trust him.

Just then, the children screamed, 'Daddy', and jumped to their feet. Sarah turned around, and saw her husband standing a few feet away. His wide smile said it all. For the first time in twenty-four hours, Sarah could breathe easy. She couldn't get up to greet him. Her legs felt too heavy.

Anthony embraced all of them, and lifted her from the chair. "It's time to go," he said, dropping a kiss on her forehead. He settled the bill at the counter, and led them outside.

The children got into the back seat, while Anthony pulled Sarah to the back of the car.

"What is it?" Sarah asked.

Anthony lifted the boot up. The car was parked by a corner, with the boot facing a wall. Nobody else could see what was inside except Anthony and Sarah.

"What is this?" Sarah screamed, as Anthony quickly covered her mouth.

CHAPTER THIRTY-ONE

"Don't shout!" Anthony said. "The money is inside the bags."

"What?" Sarah said, exasperated. "You mean you have five million in these bags?"

"Yes!" Anthony said, grinning.

"Why? What happened to Mobile Banking? They should have transferred the money to you."

"Don't you get it? What I did was illegal. This was the only way to get my money. That way, it wouldn't be traced to me."

"No, no, no! I don't like this arrangement. How do we drive around with this kind of money? It's not safe."

Anthony burst out laughing. He laughed so hard, tears spilled out of his eyes.

"What's so funny?"

Anthony got a grip on his emotions before speaking. "Darling, look at us. A middle-aged man, with his wife, and two young children. We are a typical family. No-one would look at us twice. And I am going to prove it to you."

Sarah's brows furrowed. "How do you mean?"

"We aren't going home. We are spending the weekend at Crystal Heights Hotel," he exclaimed, lifting her off her feet, and spinning her around.

Sarah was winded by the time he placed her back on her feet. "What? We don't have a change of clothes."

"That isn't a problem. We have the money to take care of that," Anthony winked at her.

Sarah took in the happiness on the face of her husband. She couldn't remember the last time she had seen him this way. He looked alive. Couldn't she just let go of her caution and enjoy this with him? The plan had worked in the end.

"You know this is a crazy plan. But come on darling, let's go have fun," she quipped, beaming.

"That's my girl," Anthony said, scooping her into his arms once more for another spin. Her warning was lost in his joyous shouts.

CHAPTER THIRTY-TWO

D apo and Deola were driving through the expressway, as they listened to the jams blasting through the radio. The station was Sound City. They mimed the lyrics with Simi, and gave high five's with Burna Boy. Soon, they were past Ajah and on their way to their destination. The sight of the trees on both sides of the road filled Dapo with relief. They rounded a corner and were finally there.

He drove some metres ahead, and parked the car by the side of the road, and they got out. Dapo welcomed the silence and serenity all around him. He allowed a smile break out on his face. Deola was staring around, entranced. He hugged her first before he opened the door, so they could pick a few things, and head to the spot.

Deola trudged behind him, as he picked his way to his destination, amongst the copse of trees he had chosen a week ago. Deola could hear the chirping of the birds, and the sounds that belonged to nature. There was a moist, earthy smell in the air. It left a sour taste in her mouth. Deola realized that they had to have the camp settled as fast as possible before it grew dark. As much as she wanted to be brave to please Dapo because of the depth of love he had for her, she didn't think she could move in the dark.

Suddenly, they came upon a clearing. It was definitely the work of nature. Where they had been miniscule space in between the trees they had walked past; here there was enough space to lay their tent, underneath the canopy of the trees.

Dapo dropped the packages, and she followed suit. She surmised that it would take them three trips to get things sorted out. Perhaps she just might enjoy it.

CHAPTER THIRTY-THREE

Yusuf was at the wheels, while Bunmi and Chima sat pensive. Their drive had been smooth. No one had stopped them. Now, they were on their way to the spot. The trees surrounded them on both sides of the expressway. They rounded the corner and Chima asked him to stop. Yusuf parked by the side of the road, and they all got out, with the batons in their hands.

Chima looked round the area. He noticed the car some metres ahead, but there was no one hanging around.

"Shouldn't we find somewhere else? It seems somebody is already here," Bunmi asked.

"No!" Chima said stubbornly. "This is a perfect spot. Any car heading to the hotel will pass through here. They would have to go through us first. If anybody, perhaps the owner of that car gives us trouble, it would be dealt with."

Bunmi shivered. He neither liked the look on Chima's face, nor the tone of his voice. It had denoted violence. He looked towards Yusuf. Yusuf gave him a hand signal to cool down. He didn't want to admit it; but at this point, he was more afraid of Chima than what it is they planned to do. It didn't help his confidence one bit.

CHAPTER THIRTY-FOUR

Anthony drove the car, while he tried to answer his children's questions. They couldn't believe that they would be spending the weekend outside the house. Today was definitely full of surprises.

"This is so cool! I can't wait to tell my friends. Daddy, does it look like Disney land?" Diana asked, for the third time.

"How many times will you ask Daddy?" Bobby questioned.

"Mind your business," Diana retorted.

It was going to turn into another fight. Sarah wasn't ready to butt in, as she covered her mouth, to stifle her laughter.

"Both of you, stop it. We are almost there. Once we go round that corner ahead, we should be there in thirty minutes," Anthony said.

"Yeah!" the children screamed, laughing, as they went back to being friends again.

Anthony joined in the laughter. The family were in a merry mood, as they rounded the corner, and came upon the men in the police uniform. They signaled at him to stop the car. He gradually brought the car to a stop, as he shared apprehensive looks with his wife.

CHAPTER THIRTY-FIVE

Deola and Dapo set the tent, and placed their sleeping bags inside. Dapo was quiet content with the fact that they had settled in, in good time. It was six p.m., but right here under the cover of the trees, it was already getting pretty dark.

"Okay, come on," Dapo nudged Deola. "Let's heat up our food. I am famished."

Deola who was trying to act brave, took the camp gas outside, while Dapo was behind with the pot. She tried to ignore the unfamiliar sounds coming from the trees. At some point, they realized they had left the lighter in the pigeon hole of the car. It meant going back to get it. Deola sighed, while Dapo laughed it off. He wanted to make it to the car and return quickly, but Deola couldn't stand to be left alone.

They turned on their big-head torchlights, and trudged on to the car. As they got closer, they turned off their torches, because they could see clearer. The car was just some metres away, when they heard the voices. They both turned towards the sound of the voices, and saw in the distance, three policemen questioning some people in a car.

Dapo knew why he did it, but he couldn't tell Deola that his Driver's license had expired. He didn't want the men to see him getting into his car and then come to him to question him. So, they remained under the cover of the trees, and he watched the scene ahead with interest, while Deola sighed loudly.

CHAPTER THIRTY-SIX

"Officer, please hold on," Anthony said. His hands shook as he retrieved the necessary papers from the pigeon hole. He didn't like the look in the man's eyes. Sarah was trembling, too scared to speak. Bobby spoke out, though.

"Daddy, is everything okay?"

He turned to face his kids, and tried hard to cover up his fears with a shaky smile. "Yes, everything is okay, my son. It's just normal police procedure. We will be on our way soon."

Anthony handed the papers to the police man, and watched anxiously as he flipped through the papers. Anthony could feel the rivulets of sweat streaming down his body.

Chima was disappointed. The man's papers were intact. His plan was to find something inappropriate, and then tax him for money. Reluctantly, he knew he had to let them go. As he looked up to speak to the man, he caught the stare that passed between the man and his wife. *What was that*, he wondered. The man turned to him and his lips trembled as he looked on in what...it flitted across his face for a second and disappeared. The wife sat stiffly, looking ahead. They were both behaving funny; like people who were...the flash of comprehension dawned on him. They were frightened! He caught the whiff of fear in the air. They were frightened, because they didn't want him to see or discover something.

The seconds stretched, before Chima threw the bombshell. "Oga, open your booth."

What?! Anthony was paralysed. He couldn't utter a word. The alarm bells were ringing in his head. No, he hadn't heard that right. A moan escaped his wife's lips. He should have gone home. What madness had brought him here! The madness of money!

"Oga, I say come down and open your booth," Chima said aggressively.

Anthony snapped out of his paralysis. "Oga, there is nothing in my boot. I'm a family man. We are heading to Crystal Height Hotel, eh. Let us go, please."

It was Yusuf who spoke this time. "Oga, if you no get anything to hide, come down."

Anthony stepped out of the car, as the thoughts whirled in his head. Perhaps he could bribe them. He could still get out of this, unscathed.

He mechanically strode to the back of the car, with the men following him behind, as if he was walking to his execution. He lifted the hood, and observed the looks on the faces of the men. The leader smiled mischievously, while the other two had their eyes grow wide. There were five Ghana must go bags, each containing one million naira.

"Open the bags," the leader ordered.

Anthony had no choice. He pulled down the zip of one of the bags. The men craned their necks and looked in. One of them shouted, while the leader and the other man turned to him. Anthony's heart raced. If he could cry, he would have gladly done so.

CHAPTER THIRTY-SEVEN

Bunmi broke the spell. "You say you be family man! Wetin you dey do with all this money?"

They had opened the other bags.

"Please," Anthony begged. "I'm not a thief. You can take one bag. That's one million. Please, just let me go."

He watched two of them wet their lips with interest. He could control this, he realized. "Please, just take the bag," he continued. He made to bring down one.

"Stop that," the leader said. "We wouldn't take one. We would take all." His eyes were filled with menace.

"No!" Anthony screamed. He couldn't let it happen. This was supposed to be his new life. They couldn't take it away from him. "Okay, take two bags," he tried again. He regretted ever stepping out of his car. He hadn't been thinking straight. He should have driven away.

The two men tried to reason with their leader. Just then the man bent down, and pulled up an object from his socks. The two men saw it before Anthony and shouted, "Chima, what are you doing?"

That was the last sentence Anthony heard. He saw the gun pointed at him a few seconds before it exploded with a shot. He fell to the ground, with a hole in his head.

CHAPTER THIRTY-EIGHT

Sarah heard the shot. She screamed and ran to the back. She saw the blood gushing out of Anthony's head a few seconds before another shot rang out. This time, it was she who was lying on the floor. Successive shots rang out, as Chima went after the kids in the car.

Suddenly, there was silence. It was eerily quiet after the loud boom of the shots. Bunmi and Yusuf stared open-mouthed.

"We agreed no guns," Bunmi shouted. "What have you done?"

"Get that money into the car, now. Let's leave before anyone comes by," Chima ordered.

They were still trying to come to terms with the order, when Yusuf said, "Who are those?" pointing ahead.

Chima and Bunmi turned to see a lady kneeling on the paved road beside the car, while a man tried to pull her up. Chima's head rang. Witnesses! They didn't need that. He didn't stop to think. He ran after them firing shots, and watched them run into the cover of the trees.

"Go after them," he cried. "Kill them! I have to secure the money."

Bunmi and Yusuf ran into the trees. They had come this far. They had to see it to the end.

CHAPTER THIRTY-NINE

Deola and Dapo had watched until the first shot rang. Dapo quickly stifled her scream by covering her mouth. From where they stood, the men couldn't see them. He brought out his phone and began videoing what was happening ahead. By the time the second shot rang out, Deola had stepped out of the cover of the trees. He had been too distraught to notice. Everything happened within a few seconds.

Dapo had his car keys in his hands. He could have driven off. But the gun shots had made him run into the bush. As they ran past their camp, he realized that this wasn't the adventure he had planned. He should have taken Deola's advice, and simply gone to the beach.

They were now running for their lives.

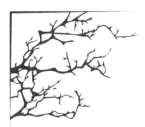

THE HUNT 1

CHAPTER FORTY

C hief Cletus smacked his lips in excitement. It was going to be a great weekend. He couldn't quite believe it, yet. He had been very restless the entire week, and wished for an escape, but it was impossible. Not under his wife's watchful eyes. Chief Cletus hated to admit that he was afraid of his wife. She loomed large like a bear, with her hawk-like eyes trailing him wherever he went. He was always looking over his back, expecting her to pounce on him at any second.

Out of the blues, her presence had been needed in the village. She had taken the first flight out of Lagos this morning, and Chief had scrambled to sort himself out. Now, a very young lady, decked in a tight mini skirt and a tube top, was seated beside him. She was old enough to be his daughter, but he didn't care. How could he? He struggled to contain himself, as she placed her hand on his right leg, running her hands all over it.

He couldn't wait to get to Crystal Heights Hotel. He had booked the reservation earlier. He turned to her, and said, "Baby, we would soon be there. I will treat you right."

She giggled, and Chief stepped up on the speedometer. He rounded the corner, and braked abruptly. What was he seeing? The young lady went into a screaming frenzy. Chief got down from his car, and took in the sight. His dinner snaked up his throat, and he threw up its contents by the side of the car. He couldn't take a second look at the scene. As he reached for his phone to call it in, he knew his plans were shattered.

CHAPTER FORTY-ONE

eola and Dapo ran past their tent. They couldn't stop because of the sounds they heard coming from behind. The men were on their tail. Dapo calculated that they could outrun them; but all that depended on how far the men were willing to chase after them. It was already pretty dark. The branches were slapping at their faces, and the sharp thorns brushed against them, but they couldn't stop. Blood trickled down Dapo's cheeks, and when Deola slipped, he hastily picked her up, held on to her hand, and resumed running. They couldn't turn on the torchlight, or the men would know where they were.

"Is there a way out of here?" Deola asked, amid short breaths.

"I have no idea," Dapo replied."

"All the plans!"

"I don't know. We have to keep running."

The both of them had no idea how long they ran. They fell down and got right up. All that Dapo thought of, was a way out of this. When Deola's hand started to slip, he held onto her tightly. It wasn't until Deola collapsed to the ground that he stopped. He wanted to shout at her to get up, but her groans reached his ears. It sounded like she was in pains. He crouched down, and held her hands. They were ice-cold. A wave of shock coursed through his veins. He had no choice but to turn on the torchlight.

Deola's face was contorted in pain, her mouth agape as she took in quick breaths, her chest was rising and falling fast. She was holding on to her side. He flashed the light on her stomach, and gasped in shock. Her shirt was soaked in blood. She had been shot.

A memory flashed in his head, of the man with the gun shooting at them, as they bolted away. Tears fell down his cheeks. This changed everything.

CHAPTER FORTY-TWO

B unmi and Yusuf were winded. They had stopped several times to catch their breath. The sweat was streaming down their bodies in rivulets; the uniform plastered to their skin.

Yusuf stopped. He couldn't breathe. "Won't these people stop? I can't continue," he complained.

He lay on the bare ground to catch his breath. Bunmi joined him on the ground, too. A couple of ticks later, Bunmi sat up.

"We are morons' o! Chima just asked us to go after them, and we did, leaving him with the money," Bunmi announced.

It was as if a veil had been lifted off Yusuf's eyes. "What if he has disappeared?"

"The more reason why we have to forget this chase and get back to the house."

"But what of them? We saw them videoing us," Yusuf asked.

"They were far away. They probably didn't get our faces. Besides, are we really going to kill them? We are not killers."

"I don't know where Chima got the gun from. Look at the trouble he has gotten us into. He is so unpredictable," Yusuf wailed.

"The more reason we have to return. We can't trust him with all that money. I still can't believe it. It's like am playing a part in a Nollywood movie. We had agreed on no guns. First, we need to return, and see if we can get some clothes from the tent they set up, so we can get rid of these uniforms. Next, we find a way out of here."

"And if he asks us about them?"

"We tell him we took care of it, but they must have dropped the phone during the chase. We have to get back to that money, or all will be for naught."

They whirled around, and began the journey back.

CHAPTER FORTY-THREE

Deola was hanging on the back of Dapo's shoulders. It was too dark to see, but Dapo groped in the darkness. He had dropped one torchlight and misplaced his car key, which he had in his hands, when the chase began. He couldn't run anymore with Deola's weight pressing on his shoulders. He trudged on, determined to keep a distance between himself and the evil men. Yes, that's what he called them. Men who could murder an entire family were evil.

His shirt was wet with Deola's blood. The smell burned thick in his throat. He couldn't cry. He was still too shocked to cry. How had things turned awry? All he needed was a way out of this damned place. The trees didn't seem to want to come to an end. He had grown tired of checking his phone for a signal. Not even an emergency call could go through. Dapo didn't think the men were still on their tail, or there would have found them, already. But, he knew he couldn't go back. There had to be a way forward.

A groan escaped Deola's lips. His arms ached. He needed to take a breather. He laid her on the ground, with her back leaning on the bark of a tree. He risked it, and turned the light on. Deola wasn't looking good. He watched her take painful breaths, and something in him broke. He couldn't breathe.

Dapo moved a step forward in anguish. He didn't want her to see him cry. That was when it happened. Dapo stepped on a patch of grass. He felt the soil give way, and he plunged right into darkness. His blood curdling scream echoed for miles.

CHAPTER FORTY-FOUR

Through the dark haze Deola had sunk into, the shrill sound of the scream pierced through her fog. That was Dapo! He was in trouble. The utter silence after the scream forced her to crawl on her knees. She couldn't see properly, so she pulled out her phone from her pocket, and switched the torchlight on. She saw the hole in the ground, and crawled cautiously. At the mouth of the hole, she pointed the phone downwards. She was too weak to scream.

Dapo lay impaled on a stick. The stick had pierced his stomach. Blood trickled from his mouth, as he gasped for breath. He was staring straight at her. She stretched her hand, willing it to reach him, but it couldn't be. Before he took his last breath, he pulled out his phone, and used his last strength to hurl it out of the pit. The motion caused the stick to penetrate deeper. He shuddered, and took his last breath.

The hours flew by. Deola knew she had one thing left to do. She crawled slowly, making her way blindly now. She had let go of her phone. Her hands searched frantically as she crawled. Eventually when she found it, her hand closed around it, and held it tightly. She died some minutes later, a sad smile plastered on her face. Indeed, it was a weekend she would never forget.

CHAPTER FORTY-FIVE

E ver since the case had been assigned to the Investigative Police Officer, Tijani, it had been a rush. Identification of the murdered family had been swift; and their bodies were currently undergoing autopsy, before being deposited in the mortuary.

The bone of contention was the motive. What could have caused the death of the family? The opened boot was a mystery. The presence of the second car was another factor in the equation. He needed answers desperately. The death had already made it to the papers and the daily news since the news broke yesterday. What shocked him the most was the pictures of the scene all over the internet? That shouldn't have happened. Somebody was going to answer for it. He had gotten calls from above. The pressure was on.

When his phone rang, he quickly clicked the accept button. His eyes grew wide at the news he heard. A tent had been discovered amongst the trees, and a car key had been found lying on the ground. He had ordered the search, and now it had yielded answers.

"I want all the available officers deployed to the scene. I want that entire area searched," he barked into the phone.

He got up, and made his way out of the office. Perhaps this case would give him the break he needed to earn a promotion, and move up the ladder. It smelt just like one.

CHAPTER FORTY-SIX

Quadri quickened his strides, as much as his short legs could carry him. The day was just breaking. The darkness was receding, and shards of daylight, though fickle, were flickering through the clouds. He welcomed the sounds as he raced through the trees. The birds were conversing amongst themselves, he thought; the sounds shrill, and welcoming, as he trudged ahead. His heart hammered as he crossed his arms. The cold was piercing, his joints were stiff. He tried to avoid touching the leaves from the trees. The liquid from the dew that morning was cold to the touch. He didn't need a drop on his body. He was cold enough!

Quadri hadn't thought to cover himself properly. As soon as he heard the first crow from the fowl in his father's compound, he slipped out of the hut, before the others stirred from their sleep. Today, he would show them that he was a man. His under-developed body belied his age. He was twenty-years-old! The right age to join the hunters! Yet, they left him behind when they went on their trips. It wasn't his fault that he was too small for his age. He had overheard the things they said behind him; that he wasn't well in the head. He knew that he picked his nose, and stared into the skies the whole day; and that whatever he found to play with, he fixated on it, until he grew tired of it. He had no friends. He loved his company and preferred to be by himself. His father never looked at him. Rather, he paid attention to Quadri's brother, who was two years younger. Today, his father was taking his younger brother on his first hunting trip. Quadri couldn't have it. He would show them what he could do. He knew where his father set his traps to catch wandering goats, and sometimes, dogs. He usually followed the men behind, without them knowing; thus he knew all the spots. He would return with the

lead animal right before they all set off. They would have no choice but
o respect him now. He squared his shoulders, and moved faster.

CHAPTER FORTY-SEVEN

Quadri came out to the clearing. So intent was he on his ruminations that he didn't see what was in front of him, until he stepped on it. At the touch, he drew back in alarm. His eyes bulged out of their sockets at the sight before him. He tried to think, but couldn't. He crept closer, and tapped the woman on the ground. She didn't move. He gasped at the sight of the blood. He drew back in shock at the sight of the man in the pit. He scratched his head, and chorused 'No, no!" repeatedly. His mind acknowledged the fact that they were dead. His plan was ruined. One thing became clear in his mind. He had to leave and feign ignorance, or he might be blamed. Quadri could picture all of them pointing fingers at him.

As he picked his way, careful not to step on anything, his gaze fell on a shiny object, held tightly in the palm of the woman. He stared at it with interest. Immediately, he knew he wanted it. He looked around frantically, checking to see if anyone was around. When he was sure, he drew closer, and tried to pry the object from her hand. Though stiff, rigor mortis at its final stage hadn't set in yet. After a few attempts, he held it in his hands, licking his lips. His outing had not been in vain. He had found a new toy. He raced into the trees. It was time to head home.

CHAPTER FORTY-EIGHT

Yusuf and Bunmi banged on the gate. They didn't let up with the pounding. Each time, they kept looking behind them. They didn't think they were followed, but they would be safer, when they got inside.

A few minutes later, Chima pulled the bolt, and opened the gate. The duo rushed in, and breathed a sigh of relief, as he bolted the gate shut.

"What happened? Where have you guys been? And whose clothes are these? Chima asked, looking perplexed.

"Let's go in first," Yusuf said.

After they had settled in, and quenched their thirst, Bunmi narrated how they stole clothes from the tent, and buried their uniforms, while Yusuf chipped in, and narrated how they walked a long distance before hitching a ride. The whole time, Chima's face held no expression.

"So, how far with the couple? Did you get them?"

"Yes," Bunmi said eagerly. He didn't think Yusuf would answer well, without giving them away. "We got the both of them. Hit them with stones on the head. They died together, wrapped in each other's embrace."

Chima looked satisfied. "No-one would be able to find them there. What of the phone?"

"We didn't see the phone on them. They must have misplaced it during the chase."

Chima sat up. "Are you sure about that? Did you search them?" His eyes darted back and forth between the two men.

"Of course, na! Don't you trust us?" Yusuf chipped in. "How about the money? Is it safe?"

Chima stared at them intensely. "Well, we have a problem."

The duo looked at each other. Their hearts thumped.

CHAPTER FORTY-NINE

"What...What is the problem?" Bunmi managed to ask.

Chima picked up his phone from the center table, pulled up some pages on his screen, and passed it to them to see.

Their eyes grew wide as they stared at the images. Words failed them.

"The money is safe. But we can't get to it, now."

"How do you mean?" Yusuf shouted. "Look at the mess we are in? The pictures are all over the internet. The police may be on our tail. We all agreed on no guns! Look at this now!" he pranced back and forth, muttering and swearing.

With a cautious voice, Bunmi spoke, "What do you mean by we can't get to the money, now? Where did you keep it?"

Chima stared them in the face, and revealed to them what he had done. They both sat back down, too nonplussed to add their voices. The deed had already been done.

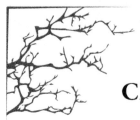

CHAPTER FIFTY

Paul stepped into Otunba Dele's living room, his expression angry. He wasn't surprised to see Otunba in a state. Otunba whirled around to face him at the sound of his footsteps.

"How could this happen? He was here yesterday? What is happening?" he asked, agitated.

Paul sat down. He was broken inside. "I honestly don't understand it myself. Who could have killed them? I have given it a lot of thought. I couldn't sleep a wink."

Otunba sat down opposite him. "My sources at the station say the boot was open. No money was found. Do you realize the implication?"

Paul shuddered. He hadn't known that. "Does it mean that Anthony was robbed, and the money stolen?"

"This is the work of my enemies. They must have been on to what we were doing. They killed him, and took the money away. That's a warning to me. My partners are wary. We don't know if Anthony revealed any information concerning what he did for us. Who can we get to move the monies to other offshore accounts? The money isn't safe anymore!"

This was a dilemma. Not only did he have to deal with the guilt that bringing Anthony in had led to the gruesome murder of his family, now, the purpose for which he was brought in was lost. The money still wasn't safe. Their enemies probably had them in the palm of their hands.

"What do we do?" he asked, his heart sinking.

CHAPTER FIFTY-ONE

Otunba Dele pressed a button. Almost immediately, three men walked in. They had the cloak of danger all around them. They were wide, heavy-set men, as a result of a lot of weight lifting. But what was more dangerous was the look in their eyes. It looked blank; void of emotion. These were dangerous men.

"These are the answers," Otunba said, pointing at them. "I have told them what to do. They must go out there and get me answers. I want to know who killed Anthony and his family. I want to know who made away with that money. Since Anthony is dead, the money is mine. And for the three of you to know that I mean business, whoever brings me the answers will be gifted that five million. Do I make myself clear?"

The leader spoke up, "Yes, Otunba. We will not disappoint you." They turned and left.

Otunba took his seat. The air was heavy with tension, as the two men sank into their thoughts.

THE HUNT 2

CHAPTER FIFTY-TWO

Ever since Pa Quadri and the group of hunters had returned, the village had been enshrouded in silence. The sight of the bodies had filled them with trepidation and fear. They had walked back, in a single file, their heads bowed. Such a gruesome death wasn't one to be cast away from the mind so easily.

Pa Quadri and his people belonged to one of the small communities scattered around the Epe area. A nearby stream supplied them with water. They relied on both poultry and crop farming to survive. However, they were untouched by the progress made in the twenty-first century. Theirs was a simple life, indeed.

Thus, the entire village mourned the gruesome death of the couple. Pa Quadri was deeply touched because the pit was meant to kill stray dogs and goats, and not humans. He sat in front of his mud hut, his eyes to the sun. Strangers hardly came here, but today, he was ready to receive them. It was inevitable.

CHAPTER FIFTY-THREE

The atmosphere was tense. They were all restless. They avoided each other, but the reproach and doubt were in their eyes. They couldn't bring themselves to speak out their minds, or all hell will break loose.

Bunmi and Yusuf were upset with Chima over the shooting. As much as they would have loved to avoid the TV and internet, they couldn't. They had to know what was happening. The issue about the money was another conversation they couldn't broach. Chima closed up whenever they tried. The two friends were equally walking on pins and needles. Bunmi blamed Yusuf for pushing Chima in the first place into this.

Chima didn't think that Bunmi and Yusuf had done the job well, or that they had searched for the phone properly, but he couldn't question them further. They were safe in this house for as long as no further information was revealed. Suddenly, a cry from below pierced the silence. He hurried down from the patio. At the landing, he crashed into Bunmi. They both rushed into the living room.

"What is it?" Chima asked Yusuf.

"They...the police have found the bodies of the man and woman in the trees."

Some minutes went past before one of them spoke. "Let's just hope that they don't find the phone you both claimed not to see," Chima said, before heading back upstairs.

CHAPTER FIFTY-FOUR

IPO Tijani stood apart. His men moved around the scene cautiously, careful not to mess the crime scene. The discovery of the tent had led them to move further into the trees. It worked, because he could hazard a guess that they were the occupants of the second car. The gunshot wound revealed that they were somehow part of the murder scene on the expressway, but how did they get here? And the pit? Did the killers dig it? If they did, it changed everything. It meant that this was a deliberate act. It was pre-meditated.

The voice of Sergeant Chibuzor cut through his thoughts. "Sir, there is a community close by. Just a few minutes' walk from here."

"What?" IPO Tijani said. "What could they possibly be doing here?" he added, chagrined.

"Most of these people can trace their roots as far back as the creation of Lagos. Some are reluctant to leave their lands, so they remain here," Sergeant Chibuzor explained.

"Well, let's pay them a visit," IPO Tijani said, with a spark in his eyes.

CHAPTER FIFTY-FIVE

Pa Quadri was seated on a bench, in front of his compound, which was at the center of the small village. The other mud huts were built around it in a circle, some distance apart, and denoting Pa Quadri's leadership; he was in a vantage position to see everything that happened around him. So when the men in uniforms made their way into his village, their voices preceding them, he was already on his feet, with three senior men, although junior to Pa Quadri, standing beside him. Pa Quadri caught sight of his younger son, Sadiq, peeping from the side of the hut. Sadiq had been sulking since the discovery of the bodies. He considered it a sign of bad luck on the first day of his hunting.

By this time, the men numbering six, had made it into the village, and were right now in front of him. A huge man, about six feet tall, with wide narrow eyes, spoke first.

"I am IPO Tijani, and these are my men," he introduced himself.

"I am Pa Quadri, the Chief and leader in this village. These are other senior men here," Pa Quadri said, pointing at the men beside him. Pa Quadri realized that the women and children had retreated into their huts. They weren't used to visitors coming into the village.

IPO Tijani stated his reason for been there. "We are coming from the scene of a crime, very close to this village. A woman lies dead from a gunshot wound, while a man equally lies dead, impaled in a pit. Do you have anything to say to us concerning this?"

Pa Quadri stood straighter. "Yes, I do."

The men in uniform stared at him now with interest.

68

CHAPTER FIFTY-SIX

"I and my men, alongside my younger son, set out this morning to go check our traps. I dug that pit and camouflaged it with patches of grass to cover the mouth. It was meant for stray animals. The pit is usually the first place we go to. When we got there, we saw the bodies. They were already dead. No one has ever come in here. This has never happened before, or I would have sealed the pit," Pa Quadri explained.

IPO Tijani took it all in. "Did you see or notice anything fishy?"

"We realized that the woman had died from a gunshot wound. There was a hole in her shirt. Everything else was pretty much the same," Pa Quadri said."

"So why didn't you call it in?"

With a firm voice, Pa Quadri replied, "We are a peaceful people. Our lives are simple. We don't leave here except to neighbouring communities' close by to trade. It wasn't our call to make."

IPO Tijani didn't like that at all. He surmised, though, that he had heard all that they knew. He pulled out his card from his wallet, and handed it to Pa Quadri. "It is your civic duty to report whatever you know. If you can't leave here, you can call me. You may have forgotten something. My number is right there. Call me if anything happens."

As he took his leave, he wondered what had made him drop his card. He trusted his instincts, though; and it had never failed him.

Axe, Spade, and Spider stood by the car, as they pondered what to do. Even though Otunba Dele's promise of the money being handed to whoever brought in the criminal should have drawn a wedge between them; they had realized they had to work together and faster due to the lack of information. They pretty much had nothing to work on.

"We need information badly," Axe enunciated. "Our hand must touch that five million."

"Yes, we have to! If not, Otunba might bring in others. The less we are, the more we stand the chance of laying our hands on the money. Five million, my brothers! Five!" he said again, counting his fingers.

Spider broke away from his thoughts. "The only way is through the police. The heat is on them. They are right now searching for clues. We must keep our ears to the ground. Once they know something, we must be the next in line."

"You have said it all. Tomorrow has got to yield something," Spade said.

They got into the car, and drove off.

CHAPTER FIFTY-SEVEN

The day dawned sunny and bright. Breakfast had been served, and the little ones were playing and rubbing their bodies on the ground. Quadri's eyes darted back and forth, like a hawk. The women had left for the market, while the men were at the farm. It hadn't been easy, waiting for them to depart, before he brought out his new toy. He hadn't brought it out to the open, for fear of it being seized, because of the mood in the village since the discovery of the corpses.

Now, the adults were away. He ran to the back of the hut excitedly, and began to burrow into the hole he had dug yesterday with his hands. Eventually, his hand touched the object. He whooped in delight and finally brought it out in the open. He unwrapped it from the piece of cloth he had used to protect it. The screen stared at him. Excitedly, he touched the screen. To his dismay, images began to move on the screen. He dropped it in alarm and drew back. What was it?

Curiosity got the better of him, and he picked it up again. He realized he enjoyed what he was seeing. Time stood. So engrossed was he, that he didn't hear the footsteps coming from behind. Sadiq peered from behind his back, and screamed at what he had seen. "Where did you get that?"

Quadri let the phone drop; his heart thumping in his chest.

CHAPTER FIFTY-EIGHT

It was mid-day. It looked like it was going to be another disappointing day. Family members and friends of the murdered family and the lovers – it had been confirmed – were firm in their belief that both parties didn't know each other. And also that they weren't involved in anything shady that would result in their death. It had been confirmed that the two lovers were to spend two nights camping. IPO Tijani couldn't believe it. Who camped in such a manner in Lagos? It was such a crazy idea to him. Another thing that bothered him was that those he had interviewed were equally quite firm in their belief that Anthony and his family couldn't have been heading to Crystal Heights Hotel. They just couldn't afford it. No one they knew lived around that area, plus that road led only to the hotel, so where else could they have been heading to, if not the hotel? And if it really was the hotel, where did the money come from? What had happened that day before their death? That was the key to solving this problem.

He sighed loudly, willing for a miracle to happen. Just then, the sound of his phone ringing filled his ears. He picked up on the second ring. A female voice spoke into the mouth piece. "Please are my speaking with IPO Tijani?"

"Yes, you are."

"I have a man here. He says his name is Pa Quadri."

IPO Tijani sat up. "Yes, I know him."

"He says he's walked several kilometres to get here. He wants you to come immediately. He has something to show you."

"Tell him I am on my way." IPO Tijani rushed out of his office.

CHAPTER FIFTY-NINE

Pa Quadri welcomed the IPO and two other men he recognized from the previous visit. He offered them the long bench. He could see the inquisitiveness in their eyes, so he went straight to the point.

"I was at the farm this morning when my younger son Sadiq came shouting for me. What he told me, and what I found out after, still astounds me. You see, my first son Quadri isn't quite right in the head, so when the time came for him to join us in the hunting, I didn't allow it. The day of the murder was supposed to be his younger brother's first day with us. Unbeknownst to us, my first son, Quadri left before us. He wanted to prove a point."

Comprehension dawned. "That means he got there before you all. He was there first," IPO Tijani said.

"Yes!"

IPO Tijani stated the obvious. "And he found something?"

Pa Quadri pulled out the phone from his pocket. IPO Tijani blinked twice. He held the phone so delicately like an egg. It was a Tecno phone. There was a warning on the screen, displaying low battery, but he touched the screen. There was a video. He played it. The video showed a woman getting out of a car, and running to the back. Suddenly there was the sound of a gunshot, and the phone tripped off. IPO Tijani was stunned.

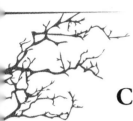

CHAPTER SIXTY

The station was a beehive of activities. The much needed miracle had surfaced in the form of the video. The loose ends had been pieced together. IPO Tijani was saddened at the death of the lovers. It was a simple case of being in the wrong place, at the wrong time. Now, he was filled with a strong desire to bring the killers to book. There had to be a way to track them. What drove him nuts was that they had the gall to operate with the police uniform. Tijani prided himself with the fact that he was one of the clean men on the police force. He had sworn to protect the lives of the Nigerian citizens, and that got him up from his bed each morning. He must nail the killers.

He was in talks with his men, when one of the sergeants rushed in. His look spelt doom. Tijani's brows lifted in consternation.

"Sir," the sergeant blurted.

"What is it?" he asked.

The sergeant handed Tijani his phone. The look on the IPO's face went from incredulity, to confusion, and then to anger. He had failed to fish out the mole. The video was now available on social media. This spelt a greater headache. IPO Tijani couldn't suppress a sigh.

CHAPTER SIXTY-ONE

When the video was uploaded onto a popular gossip website 9jatalks, by an unknown source, it was viewed immediately by thousands of people. Within a short while owing to the nature of the video, other sites were uploading it onto their websites, after acknowledging the host. It began trending on Twitter with millions of comments. Social media was on fire!

The buzz was transferred to the electronic media as major talk shows on radio picked it up. TV stations included it in their news bulletins, although parts of the video were not shown. Anger was rife over the senseless killings. The video was misinterpreted and the police force received a major backlash. Radio stations were overwhelmed with calls describing the unjust acts of the police force and their constant harassment. Social media dragged the police force through the gutters. Human rights activists were hurriedly called in to TV programs to give their take on the matter. The thought that the video could be misleading didn't cross the minds of the general public.

In the midst of the backlash, the police public relations officer, Mrs. Nkiru Okoro had to come out with a statement, refuting the claim that the men in the video were their men. In order to get to the bottom of the situation, she asked that the public assist the police in tracking the men down. As for the complaints concerning the conduct of police officers, investigations would be made, and a proper restructuring and accountability would be enforced within the force.

Within twenty-four hours, the status quo had changed. It was now a hunt! A hunt to find the killers!

CONSEQUENCES

CHAPTER SIXTY-TWO

Ever since they had seen part of the video on TV and on their phones, none of them had said a word. How could they? What had seemed perfect from the get go had turned sour! And it was all because of one person's action. But Bunmi and Yusuf were afraid to speak out. Chima had a dangerous temper, plus they didn't know if he had disposed of the gun. They hadn't asked him. He had always been a step ahead of them from the first day they met at Mama Nonso's bar. They had felt drawn to his aloofness and self-indulgence in himself. Both saw in him a confidence they could never have, and a mindset to reach for things and grab it.

It had started with a few drinks, until he accepted them into his fold, and invited them into his house. Over a period of time, they began passing the night at his place. Chima shed his thick skin, and became quite free with them; but they always knew, that he would be the one to do greater things amongst the trio.

Of course, he had succeeded. Their faces were all over the different forms of media. If only they had the money within reach, it would have been a sweet salve to their soul.

Indeed, something great had happened. And it was going to be the death of them.

CHAPTER SIXTY-THREE

Chima lay on the bed, his eyes staring at the ceiling, intently. He hadn't stepped out of the room the whole day. He avoided Bunmi and Yusuf as much as he could. Their stares were like daggers. It could plunge into him at any time.

Where had he gone wrong? He had agreed with them not to use a gun, but on that last day at work, he had had a change of heart. It was the company's policy to have the security armed because of two earlier breakins. As he signed out that morning, and made to drop the gun, he found out he couldn't. It felt like a cashmere sweater on a rainy day. It was his covering. He left the factory that morning with the gun, consequences at the back of his mind.

Everything had happened in a flash. The sight of the money had filled his senses, shrinking away his self-control, and forcing through that power he had always kept at bay. He felt it as he pulled the trigger each time he took the shots. He had killed for that money. Whatever was happening now won't sink him. And neither will Bunmi and Yusuf; even though they had lied to him about killing the lovers. He had seen it in their eyes. They had accepted defeat. Well, certainly not him.

He knew what to do. Once they turned in for the night, he would make his way out of here, and get his money. This wouldn't be the end of him.

CHAPTER SIXTY-FOUR

Baba Tolu was on the brink of losing his mind. Ever since he had noticed the gun hadn't been returned, he had forgotten how to breathe. The days were torturous, the nights a complete nightmare. As the supervisor, he should have reported it. The thought of it had made him shed weight overnight.

But how could he? That look in Chima's eyes, and his general aloofness had stopped him. He didn't want to get in Chima's bad book. For three days, he had waited for Chima to return with the gun. He had even gone to check him at his place, after checking for his address in the form he had filled when applying for the job, but he wasn't there.

But all that had changed last night after watching the nine p.m. news. He knew that face belonged to Chima. He still couldn't come to terms with the fact that Chima had killed them all. For what reason?

Now, he was in a dilemma. His job was on the line whether he spoke or not. The police were asking for information. His daughter had informed him this morning before he left for work, about the hashtags online. There was a hunt for the killers.

What could he do? He had to do the right thing. Perhaps something gallant; and maybe Mama Tolu would start paying attention to him, again. That thought gladdened his heart, and loosened the grip of fear. What gave him further courage was something that had been tinkling in his mind since last night. Some ten days back, he had been looking through the roster when he felt he needed to confirm the dates with Chima before heading home. Chima was busy on the phone and didn't hear him approach. He caught the last few words – an address at Ajah – something about an Uncle travelling. Could it be where he was?

Baba Tolu made a decision. He will pay a visit to the police station after close of work by six p.m.

CHAPTER SIXTY-FIVE

Since the man Baba Tolu had been questioned, it had been a frenzy of activities at the station. After consultations with his team, it was decided that they storm the place that night. It was 6:45 p.m. With the fear of the mole hanging over his head, IPO Tijani tried as much as he could to keep his team in one room, and their phones monitored. He couldn't afford the general public getting this information before they stormed the place. He hoped he had being enable to forestall any disclosure.

A team on a bike was sent to stake the place, while Tijani prepared his men. They would move in a convoy of six police vehicles. He wouldn't leave any stone unturned. He would bring in the men tonight.

CHAPTER SIXTY-SIX

Chima slipped out of the house as Yusuf and Bunmi slept off in their rooms. He cast a last glance at the house as he walked away. It would be the last time he would be here. He hurried to his destination, casting glances back and forth. His face was shielded by the hooded shirt he had on, plus the failing light as the darkness crept in, protecting him.

He took a bike and arrived at the destination, but nobody was there. He stood shocked, as he took in his disappointment. He directed the bike rider to a different location. To his chagrin, he met a closed door. No one in the compound had seen the occupant of the room in the last two days.

Now, Chima's heart beat raced. This couldn't be happening. He had been too sure about this. He had gotten rid of his phone after the operation but he knew the number. Chima ran to a call center. He had no other choice but to show his face more than he wanted to. The voice on the other end informed him that the number was unavailable. He cursed loudly, and the lady stared at him. He was drawing unnecessary attention.

Chima stalked out of the shop, blind rage seething inside. What could he do? A thought lashed at him. Perhaps Bunmi and Yusuf might know something he didn't. He had to return. He didn't like it one bit.

CHAPTER SIXTY-
SEVEN

As Spider took the call, Axe and Spade watched Spider's eyes bulge out of their sockets. A slow smile spread across his face as he ended the call. The others waited anxiously for him to speak.

"We have them. Our source has just revealed the address. The police will be moving out in fifteen minutes. We can get there before them if we move now."

They needed no further encouragement. The men got into the car, with Axe at the wheel, and Spider in the passenger seat. Spider envisaged the five million naira. He couldn't wait to get his hands on it. Otunba Dele will most certainly be pleased.

CHAPTER SIXTY-EIGHT

Bunmi and Yusuf were roused from their sleep, as the men in uniforms barged into their rooms. It had been easy gaining entry into the house due to the gate Chima had left open when he left. Bunmi and Yusuf were not aware that Chima had left the house. So when they were questioned about his whereabouts after being handcuffed, they were shocked and had no answer to give.

IPO Tijani was disappointed. He wanted the man who had drawn the shots. He wanted him here, handcuffed. He instructed some of his men to take the two culprits to the station, while he stayed behind with the rest. He wanted to be here to welcome the shooter when he walked through the gate.

CHAPTER SIXTY-NINE

The trio were approaching the house when they heard the sound of sirens, and the approaching headlights from a distance. Axe quickly shut the engine, while they bent down, so they couldn't be seen. After the cars swept past, they raised their heads up, and rushed out of their cars.

"Oh, no, no, no!" Axe bellowed, frustration written all over his face.

"Damn this traffic! If not for it, we would have gotten here before them, eh," Spade joined in.

Spider stayed mute, his mind swirling with thoughts. They couldn't possibly attack the police station. Things could go wrong. What could he do? He couldn't afford to disappoint Otunba Dele. He got back into the car, and the others followed suit. It wasn't wise to stay here.

Anger marked their features as Axe drove away, taking them out of the area. Spider sat deep in thought, his brows furrowed in concentration, as he mulled what next to do, when he observed a man walking ahead. The street lights revealed his quick, measured strides. What caught Spider's attention was the hood over his head. What was he trying to hide?

Their car went past the man in the street, and Spider turned to take a look at him. The man raised his face up for a tad bit. Spider gasped in surprise. He didn't stop to think. He opened the door, as the car was in motion, and touched his feet to the ground, surprising his men in the car. A look of alarm crossed the face of the man on the street. They both looked at each other, weighing themselves.

It happened within seconds. Chima shoved his hands into his pocket, and came out with a gun. He pointed it at Spider, as Spider ran towards him. The shot rang out, as Spider threw him down to the ground.

CHAPTER SEVENTY

The two men were placed in different questioning rooms. Inspector Tolu was the man in charge of questioning them. He ambled into the room, and sat himself across Bunmi. The preliminary introductions were made before the main questions began.

"Why did you kill them?"

"We weren't supposed to kill anybody. It was meant to be just a robbery. Chima had the gun. We weren't aware of the other couple in the trees."

"So why did you kill the man and his family since you say it was a robbery? What did you take from them?"

"We took his money. Chima killed them. Please, I had nothing to do with that?"

"How much was it?"

"It was five million naira."

"Where is Chima?"

Hatred swept across Bunmi's features. "I don't know."

"Where is the money?"

Bunmi stared at him, too heart-broken to speak.

CHAPTER SEVENTY-ONE

Yusuf was crying loudly. He stretched his cuffed hands towards Inspector Tolu. "Please, we didn't mean to kill anybody. It wasn't us. It was Chima," he begged.

"Where is Chima?"

"I don't know. He must have left while we were sleeping. The bastard! He betrayed us."

"Where is the money?"

Yusuf burst out crying. He mentioned a name and address. Inspector Tolu burst out of the room, asking for IPO Tijani.

CHAPTER SEVENTY-TWO

S pider was seething with rage. He held onto his shoulder as the blood dripped down. Chima had shot him in the shoulder, right before he brought him down. He was too angry to take care of it, now.

Axe and Spade bundled Chima into a room inside Otunba Dele's house. Otunba and Paul were present. Paul lunged at him, and punched him in the face. "Why did you kill them? Why did you kill them?" he screamed.

The others joined in, throwing punches at him. Chima was a bloody mess. He hadn't seen this coming. In between the blows, he revealed what he had done. Otunba Dele was disgusted. "So where is the money?" he asked.

"I don't have it. The person I kept it with has disappeared. I was returning from there, when I saw the police vehicles, and was later picked up by your men," he managed to say.

"You had no right to kill them. You could just have taken the money and let them be. Spider, do what you want with him," Otunba said, as he walked away with Paul.

"Where is the money?" Spider asked, veins standing out in his forehead. "I'm going to kill you. Where is the money?"

Chima's screams echoed round the room, but no help was forthcoming.

CHAPTER SEVENTY-THREE

Mama Nonso had taken what Chima had done as a second chance at life. Out of the blues, Chima had come to her bar, with five bags containing money. He wanted her to keep it safe until he came for it.

Mama Nonso had stayed back in the shop. She had to take care of the bags, and that meant not letting it out of her sight. When she watched the video on TV, she realized the situation she had gotten into. But surely, she could make something out of it. She bought jerry cans, and stuffed it with the money. Then, she hired a bus to take her to GOD IS GOOD MOTORS Park. She claimed the jerry cans contained palm oil. She was on her way to Imo state.

Mama Nonso had always known that she came from Imo state, but she had never been there. With this money, she needed a new location. Besides, who would notice her? There was nothing to stand her out. She was simply one of the millions of people, walking around with ordinary faces, leaving ordinary washed-out lives. No one will turn to give her a second look; and this was why it would work.

This was a second chance at life. She had never done anything useful. But with this money, she could live a better life, even open a better business. She had equally been pondering something. With her money, she could find a way to adopt a child; a boy. He could be the son she never had. She would call him Nonso, too. She could do it.

The future certainly looked bright.

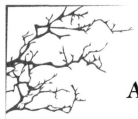

About The Author

TRACEY CHIZOBA FLETCHER is a Nigerian-born Briton based in Lagos, Nigeria. She is a writer, voice over artist, and an editor. She was the winner of the Afritondo Alternative Ending Competition and has a short story published on their platform.

---

1. https://pabpub.com/user/tracey1990/dp/dpmsO1.jpg

Printed in Great Britain
by Amazon